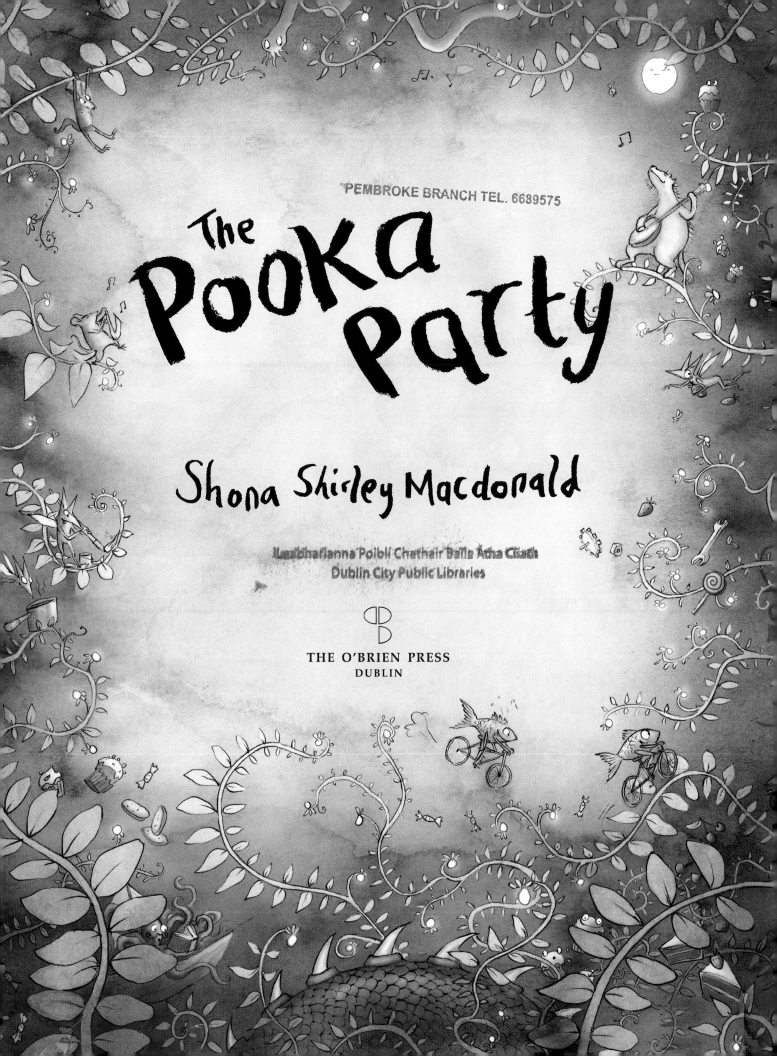

The Pooka Party

Shona Shirley Macdonald

THE O'BRIEN PRESS
DUBLIN

Now

listen very carefully,

I'm going to tell you about a

magical creature

called ...

the Pooka!

It's a shapeshifter,

which means it can take the shape of a goat ...

a dog

a cat

an eagle

a horse

a snail

a hare

or even a person!

It likes living alone
in the mountains,
where it spends its time ...

fixing things,

making soup,

painting, singing, gardening and dancing

(all at the same time).

But one day, suddenly these things were
not fun anymore.

The Pooka was lonely.
It hadn't seen its friends in ages.

So it turned itself into a snail

and hid away for a long time ...
until it had an idea.

Why not have a party?

(Deer FelloW Beeings,
I invite yoo to a
Pooka party, ther
will be mOOsic
and lotz of cake.
Address: By the
woterfall and near
the hOOj bowlder.
Time: Midnite.)

The Pooka baked cakes,

put up decorations,

combed its beard

and waited ...

and waited ...

and waited ...

but no one came.

The Pooka was so
sad and tired

that it curled up ...

14

and went to sleep.

So it didn't hear the door creeeeaaaaking open.

Everyone had come after all!

Soon they were so busy chatting
and playing music

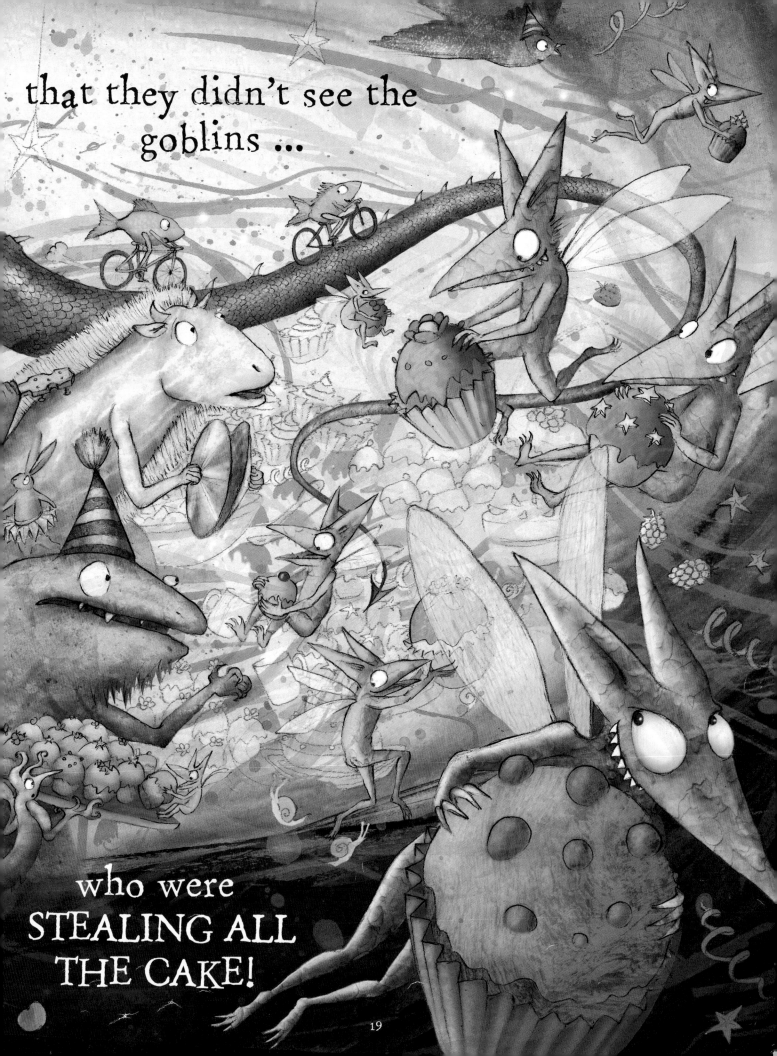

that they didn't see the goblins ...

who were
STEALING ALL
THE CAKE!

'After them!' cried the Pooka.

Everyone dashed outside and tried to catch the goblins.

But instead it turned into a
MIGHTY CAKE BATTLE!

It got so noisy that they woke up the Moon,

who was not happy.

Sorry!

The Moon made the
goblins say sorry. And they
all went back to the Pooka's house,

where the Pooka gave them delicious, sparkly soup.

The goblins too – as long as they promised to be good.

When the party was over,
everyone flew,
scampered or
galloped home,

30